DEDICATED

With love and gratitude, I dedicate this book to my forever sister, Erin.

In her passing, I promised her I would live my best life. The motivation in creating this came from her. My sister, I love you and thank you for showing me the gift of life.

To my other two life's heroes, my children: Lauren and Will.

For my children for fully supporting me and loving me in all that I do. For allowing me freedom to be myself and live a full life. I love you both with all of my heart and thank you both for showing me unconditional love. You are my world.

Finally for my dad. My absolute rock, my strength, and my guiding light. Thank you for never giving up on me and for always being there.

My heroes. I love you all.

DESIGN YOUR BEST SELF

"Being your authentic self is the ultimate secret to happiness in life!"

Sheri Fink

In my journey to finding happiness I encountered a lot of pain. I had no idea that for a long time in my journey I did not know how to live. It was only in true suffering did I look for an easier way. I knew life had to be easier, I knew no human should suffer this much and I looked at the world and shouted loudly I just want to be happy! Please show me the way.

In that moment of surrender something profound happened... I stopped fighting. I gave up on the person I was, and I started to search for who I really was. No mask, no **fakeness** , no pretending, no bullshit, no trying to impress everyone, I just wanted to be me. Unapologetically me! Free, happy, joyful, innocent, in love with me! Was that too much to ask? Was I in there? Was I possible?

Somewhere deep in my soul I knew there was this powerful human just wanting to know how to be!

This book is a short version of some of the ways that changed my life, the things I learned, the things I had to unlearn, and the beauty that lies within self discovery.

If I can honestly give you my greatest wisdom it is this... never be afraid of who you are, you have so much power, beauty and intelligence that, if you could only scratch the surface, you will find absolute abundance in the wealth of your humanness. We are all such powerful individuals, our uniqueness is incredible, all we have got to do is tap into that power, find out who we truly are and create a life of purpose that inspires and motivates us to get up every day and be our absolute best selves! There only is one version of you so let's get stuck in and design your greatness that you know you want the world to see!

ONE
LOOKING AT YOUR PAST SELF

One of the most important yet neglected life skills is to look back on past iterations of yourself and take note of how much you've changed, what exactly has changed, and what you can learn from the process of examining who you were in contrast with who you are right now.

It is too easy to dismiss the past and claim that forgetting about it will set you free. Forgetting the past won't set you free — it will only cause you to neglect a necessary step in self-help and repeat what you were unwilling to reflect on and learn from. *You will need to face the memories and take everything that you can that will help you move forward, one small step at a time.*

If you've grown at all, looking back on your past selves will make you cringe.

Whenever I reflect on the way I thought, reacted, and dealt with my emotions as an early 20-something, I cringe. Sometimes I feel disgusted towards certain things about my past selves, and other times I laugh. But most importantly, I can see that changes have occurred and for the better.

As you evolve, you'll appreciate how far you've come and looked at the past with appreciation instead of regret.

When you look back with the intent to understand rather than condemn, your past selves will have less power over you. You will begin to see why you reacted the way you did as you gain insights on how your reactions have changed over time.

As you mindfully examine the past, you will become more aware of how much more you could evolve, given how much you've discovered about the differences between your past selves and your current self.

You aren't meant to look back and be overly despairing at the way you handled certain events and setbacks. However, you also aren't meant to look back and be completely satisfied either.

You will find that the past was full of embarrassing, uncomfortable, awkward moments, but also understand that you dealt with certain things in the only way you knew how to at the time, considering the constraints you were facing.

But one thing is for certain — the more you are willing to be upfront about your past actions, the more you're able to see how you have evolved and will continue to evolve in more constructive and mindful ways in the years to come.

SELF HELP TIPS ON LOOKING AT YOUR PAST SELF

- **You are sufficient, and it's alright to be adequate.**

Permitting myself the appreciation I merit is presumably the hardest thing I've done at any point. I generally believed that there was something more I could have contributed to specific circumstances. Giving the best of yourself to a person or thing is actually all you can do, and you can't give a greater amount of something that you don't have. When I acknowledged that, the tyrannical commitment I had consistently felt appeared to have evaporated. Stop worrying about the future.

- **That one test grade isn't going to ruin your life.**

Trust me. Failing that one GCSE Biology test in secondary school will not ruin your life or college career. I actually had forgotten about it up until this point, which speaks for itself.

- **Stress over how you need to address yourself, not how others anticipate that you should be addressed.**

I felt like a greater part of my secondary school vocation was centered around others' opinion of me. I had arrived at my final year and contemplated internally, "Why do I mind to such an extent? For what reason am I so worried about others' assessments of me instead of my own?" Basically, your bliss does not rely upon other's opinion about you. By the day's end you have yourself in the entirety of its magnificence, and you need to address yourself in the manner you will be most joyful.

- **Don't be afraid to say what's on your mind.**

Raising my hand in class and speaking my mind in front of 20-something kids was not the kind of student I was. **I had constant anxiety over what people thought of me**, so I would sit in a bundle of self criticism, worried about everyone's opinions of me. I should have just reframed and saw the anxiety was the teacher within me trying to teach me to have confidence in my voice.

I just merely listened and, from that, formed my own values and opinions. But growing up and putting myself out there not only showed me that other people not black and white. All the grey areas lie in millions of other people's minds, so speaking up and sharing your own thoughts is the only way you are going to learn and develop your opinions and beliefs.

- **It's OK to ask for help.**

Really, it is! No one expects you to be perfect and know the answer to everything, especially when it comes to handling tricky situations. You should never have to carry that weight all by yourself. Actually, my biggest revelation…. People love to help others!

- **If you're not happy with something, do something about it.**

It appears to be sufficiently straightforward; however, how frequently would you say you are truly forthright with somebody about an issue you have with them? Seldom. It's generally simpler to contain it and vent to a companion later than it is to address it straightforwardly. Yet, openness is absolutely vital in any relationship, regardless of whether it's heartfelt or simply companions, romantic or solely platonic. You can't anticipate that someone should know what is pestering you on the off chance that you never advise them. What's more, trust me, after you spread everything out on the table and open up, you can continue forward to whatever is next without agonizing over that issue emerging once more.

- **Stop making excuses for yourself.**

"I'm generally so busy", "I totally disregarded that,", "I just didn't have the time." Quit lying, we as a whole realise you were too distracted on Netflix and decided to stay away from your duties. You can coast past them for a brief period, however managing **them and communicating clearly with love** will make it simpler to deal with later on.

- **Get more involved.**

Don't shy away from opportunities that put you out of your comfort zone! It builds character, and you end up learning more about yourself than you initially thought you would.

- **It's alright to leave certain circumstances.**

I generally struggled permitting myself the opportunity of leaving an issue that I could not do much else for. It is troublesome leaving a circumstance with the expectation of it improving later on, however it **is imperative to recall that occasionally with the end goal for things to improve you need to leave and allow it to relax.** Stop people pleasing!

- **Don't forget to put yourself first**

I know it's easier to let someone else take the reins in social situations, but don't forget that you have a voice too, and it matters! You have the ability to do what you want in this life, do not let that go to waste simply because you are afraid of not agreeing with someone.

- **Make peace with your past.**

You may have to invest a little energy when contemplating why you may be stuck in the past. Do you feel like you aren't deserving of pushing ahead? Perhaps you hurt somebody, and you think remaining stuck in the past is your discipline?

Is it true that you are clutching resentment since you think your annoyance reduces somebody else's life? Perhaps somebody hurt you, and you are apprehensive as continuing onward would mean what they did wasn't unreasonably terrible?

Once in a while, choosing not to move on is a simple method to divert yourself from the present. On the off chance that you get yourself troubled now; you may be enticed to romanticise how much more joyful you were "back then." Maybe you review every one of the beneficial things that occurred in a past relationship, and you sift through every one of the contentions and issues that drove you to separate.

- **Focus on the lessons you learned.**

Contemplating the shamefulness or the repulsiveness of an occasion will keep you stuck. To mend, you may have to invest some energy zeroing in on current realities, not the feelings.

Walk yourself through a difficult memory, and consider current realities, not your pain. Recall where you were sitting, what you were doing, who was there, and what had befallen you. Then, at that point consider the exercises you gained from enduring that agonising thing or for bearing that troublesome experience. Probably the best life exercises can be gained from the hardest occasions you've persevered. So, whether you write in a diary or you replay the story inside your head, work on going through the subtleties as though you were a storyteller who just relates current realities. Doing this a couple of times can assist with assuaging the experience.

IN CONCLUSION

Accept Your Past, Embrace Your Present, Plan for Your Future

Declining to choose not to move on isn't tied into overlooking the things that occurred. All things considered, it frequently requires embracing and tolerating your encounters so you can embrace the here and now. So, perceive the enthusiastic cost that abode on something is taking on you, and afterward allow yourself to push ahead.

On the off chance that somebody has violated you, this may include rehearsing absolution. This doesn't intend to "forgive and forget." You may need to adhere to your choice to have no contact with the individual. However, centre around pardoning by relinquishing the hurt or outrage you feel toward that individual.

Your vision of things to come ought to be about who you need to become - not who you used to be. So, while you can consider the previous enough to gain from it, try to relinquish whatever outrage, disgrace, or blame is keeping you away from pushing ahead. Forgiveness is key to being free. I say these affirmations to release the blocks or resentments I have carried and work on dissolving my own internal script I have created around that person-place or thing,

I choose to forgive this person and set them free

I choose to let go of anything that does not serve me well

SET YOURSELF FREE FROM YOUR PAST

What story in your mind is holding you back?

Write it all down, however you wish to....

Ask yourself...

Is this story, experience, belief, serving my best self today?

Now, just renounce it with forgiveness affirmations!

Choose to set your past free...

These allow me to let go and release what I'm holding onto, and in return allows more good feelings into my life.

Remember the golden rule of the mind... what we focus on we receive, so today I choose to focus on better thoughts for me.

TWO

CHANGING YOUR INTERNAL SCRIPT

Your script is the story you have created about how the world works and your place in it; it is your attempt at making sense of the world. Your script forms from your earliest days, through a combination of sensations, impressions, feelings and perceptions, through to verbal and non-verbal messages from your parents as you grow older.

Together with parental influence, your script is also shaped by the beliefs and values of the culture and society you were immersed in as a child. Your script is also shaped by the conclusions and decisions you arrived at during childhood.

As you grow, your script becomes an unconscious life plan. Although the script is outside of your awareness, it still exhibits a massive influence over the way you live your life as an adult. Indeed, if you are in doubt whether or not you are in a script, it is safe to assume that you probably are!

Imagine a situation where you feel obligated to do something – yet you strongly disagree with it. Perhaps you were told to sell a new product to a trusted account. But you think the product is badly flawed. Due to fear of reprisals from your boss, or embarrassment in front of your peers, you feel afraid to bring up your concerns. When you talk about it publicly, you express enthusiasm. But to yourself you think, "this situation stinks." That's your Inner Script.

Inner Scripts place you in a "no-win" situation. As far as you are concerned, you lose face if you talk to your boss, and you lose face if you present the product to your customer. *So what should you do?*

The right course of action is to communicate your concern to your boss using a technique that will trigger his desire to help you, rather than a defensive reaction. Inner Scripts provide you with a mechanism to do this.

The content of your life seems to flow seamlessly but it is more of a succession of still frames, like a movie. The film moves through the projector and displays as a coherent whole, but we know that it is a series of distinct, still frames. When you stop the motion and freeze the frame, the movie becomes a slide show.

Similarly, our lives are a series of "moments" that flow together. We tend to extract one frame here, another one there, and fabricate stories about them. Good ones are called "show stoppers." Someone may suddenly take issue with something that is happening and... the brakes go on. Suddenly, there's a story to process. "Why did you say that to me? What did you mean by that?" Or, "that reminds me of the time ..."

SELF HELP TIPS ON CHANGING YOUR INTERNAL SCRIPT

- Spend some time reflecting on your core beliefs and where they come from. Permit yourself to be a witness to this and to observe without judgment.
- Write a list of 10 things that you feel passionate about or inspire joy in your life. This is an opportunity to connect with your 'true voice' and to begin to shape the life that you want.
- Write a list of 10 things that you would love to do if you were not held back by fear or limiting self-beliefs.
- Set yourself three small tasks each month that will help you to embody your new narrative, for example: "I will prioritise my self-care in my day".
- Write your life story as if you are already living it. You can do this in as much detail as you like, but the more you can visualise the life that you want, the more likely it is that you will achieve it.

NOTE: *Observing the root of our belief system is one of the most powerful things we can do for ourselves, to create the life we want. Starting with small steps makes this a fully realistic transformation.*

DESIGN YOUR OWN SCRIPT

Write down:
How do I want to feel..?

'

Write down:
How would I like to act and respond to life?

Write down:
How can I project daily as my best self?

Well done, you.
You're doing great!
Brenda x

THREE
FORGIVENESS

When someone you care about hurts you, you can hold on to anger, resentment, and thoughts of revenge — or embrace forgiveness and move forward.

Who hasn't been harmed by the activities or expressions of another? Maybe a parent continually scrutinised you growing up, an associate or school frenemy bullied or belittled you, a partner had an unsanctioned romance. Or on the other hand, possibly you have had a horrendous encounter, been harmed in a physical or emotionally abusive way by someone close to you or abused in a traumatic event.

These injuries can leave you with enduring sensations of outrage and harshness — even retaliation.

In any case, on the off chance that you do not practice absolution, you may be the person who suffers the most beyond all doubt. By accepting pardoning, you can likewise accept harmony, expectation, appreciation, and bliss. Consider how absolution can lead you down the way of physical, enthusiastic, and profound prosperity.

What is Forgiveness?

Forgiveness implies various things to various individuals. Psychologists define forgiveness as a conscious, deliberate decision to release feelings of resentment or vengeance toward a person or group who has harmed you, regardless of whether they actually deserve your forgiveness..... forgiveness does not mean forgetting, nor does it mean condoning or excusing offences.

However absolution can reduce its grasp on you and assist with liberating you from the control of the individual who hurt you. **Pardoning** can even prompt sensations of getting sympathy and empathy for the person who hurt you.

Forgiveness does not mean neglecting or pardoning the mischief done to you or making up with the individual who caused the damage. Absolution brings a sort of harmony that assists you with going on with life. You can detach emotionally through forgiveness by healing that part of your life and what you are letting go of is everything you are still holding onto inside of you, because that anger is a huge part of what is holding you back in the present.

How to Forgive Yourself

Making peace and moving forward is often easier said than done. Being able to forgive yourself requires empathy, compassion, kindness, and understanding. It also requires you to accept that forgiveness is a choice.

Whether you are trying to work through a minor mistake or one that impacts all areas of your life, the steps you need to take to forgive yourself will look and feel the same

Focus on your feelings: One of the initial phases in figuring out how to pardon yourself is to zero in on your feelings. Before you can push ahead, you need to recognise and deal with your feelings

Recognise the mistake out loud: If you commit an error and keep on battling with releasing it, recognise it so anyone can hear what you gained from the slip-up, When you give a voice to the considerations in your mind and the feelings in your heart, you may liberate yourself from a portion of the weights. You additionally engrave to yourself what you gained from your activities and results.

Consider each mix-up a learning experience: Think about each "mistake" as a learning experience that holds the way to pushing ahead quicker and all the more reliably later on. Instead see what you can learn from the experience.

Allow yourself to put your errors in a box: If you commit an error yet struggle to forget about it, imagine your considerations and sentiments about the misstep going into a holder, for example, a jar or box.

Then, at that point, disclose to yourself that you are setting this to the side until further notice and will get back to it if and when you are ready to deal with it.

Discuss with your inward pundit: Journaling can assist you with understanding your internal pundit and foster self-empathy.

Get clear about what you need: If the slip-up you made hurts someone else, you need to decide the best strategy. Would you like to converse with this individual and apologise? Is it essential to accommodate them and offer peace?

In case you are vacillating about what to do, you should think about offering peace. This goes past saying sorry to an individual you have harmed. All things being equal, attempt to fix the slip-up you've made.

SELF HELP TIPS ON FORGIVENESS

- **REMEMBER THAT EVERYBODY MAKES MISTAKES, INCLUDING YOU!**

We are all human and therefore, we are all prone to making mistakes. Nobody is perfect.

The good thing about making mistakes is that we can learn from them. If someone is begging for your forgiveness, it could be because they have seen the error of their ways and that in itself, is something to acknowledge.

- **FORGIVE – NOT FOR THEIR BENEFIT, BUT YOUR PEACE OF MIND!**

Put yourself first! Forgive for your own sake – not theirs! They do not even have to know you have forgiven them. The impact this will have on your mental wellbeing will be so beneficial; how can you move forward if you are still looking to the past?

- **REMEMBER A TIME WHEN YOU WERE FORGIVEN**

As I said, no one is perfect, and we have all made mistakes. Take inspiration from someone that found it in themselves to forgive you once upon a time. You get to be the bigger person now. Rise above it!

- **REMEMBER WHAT YOU LIKED ABOUT THEM**

If you want to forgive someone that was once a friend, family member, or partner – there must, at some point, have been something you liked about them. Try and think about them in a positive light – maybe they made you laugh, or were generous, or interesting to talk to. Love is the key to forgiveness, and forgiveness is the key to happiness.

- **EVERY TIME YOU THINK OF THEM, BREATHE DEEPLY AND SMILE**

A meditation of sorts. When you picture the person you want to forgive, try not to think about how they hurt you, but think of them and smile. You can even say the words 'I forgive you as you do this. If you repeat this every day for five minutes, you will eventually free your mind of any negative thoughts, and make way for new, positive ones!

- **UNDERSTAND YOU WON'T BE ANGRY FOREVER, SO WHY HOLD ON TO SOMETHING THAT IS GOING TO GO AWAY ANYWAY?**

Time is a healer, and inevitably, feelings of anger or pain will eventually fade as you move on with your life. Knowing this valuable piece of information, doesn't it make sense to free yourself of this burden sooner rather than later? Life is too short to waste time hating people.

- **BE KIND INSTEAD OF RIGHT**

Two wrongs do not make a right. Just because someone has behaved badly, does not mean you have to stoop to their level and retaliate or respond aggressively. Be the bigger person. Be kind, not only to them but to yourself. Just look at Katie Kindness – she knows the drill:

"We would always recommend distancing yourself from people who make you feel bad. This doesn't mean you have to hate them or hold a grudge. Just work on other friendships, surround yourself with people who make you feel good, and keep in mind that people can change, and you can forgive."

-Katie Kindness

DESIGN A MENTAL FORGIVENESS BOX

What things would you like
to be forgiven/forgiven of

Cut out the black square below!

This is the lid for your forgiveness box — use glue or tape to put a lid on your
box to leave these things behind!

I forgive these things
And
Release them from me...

Namaste

FOUR
ACCEPTING YOUR PAST

"Accept, then act. Whatever the present moment contains, embrace it as if you had chosen it. This will miraculously change your whole life."

-Eckhart Tolle

Being present. It sounds so simple, right? But too often we are taken out of the present moment. Our heads get cluttered with the 'mind chatter' of yesterday, broken memories, and anxieties and fears of what is to come; all the while, we look past the beauty and simplicity of the present—this moment, right now.

It has taken me years to learn how to live presently. The turning point in my life came in two stages, firstly when my marriage broke up, I lost my home, my career, my independence, my income, my safety net and, what felt like, my worth as a person. In my 40s I was left alone and vulnerable and had no idea how I was meant to create an independent life by myself and look after my two teenagers.

Secondly a few months after my marriage fell apart my youngest sister died, she died a long painful death by addiction. Her death completely destroyed my world. I have never experienced pain like this, I had no idea how to cope, I was just completely broken. She was my best friend, my soul mate and my absolute rock. She was gone, at 32 she was taken and through her death came my great awakening. I finally realised I have life, I am alive, I have to live and make her proud because in her last words to me she said, "You have the power to live, please help others by sharing my story and do not let anyone suffer like me. Use your voice and help others heal." WOW what an empowering moment! I looked around me and in my pain and hysteria and I knew something had to change. I had to change. I had to learn how to live, all by myself, how to do this on my own. Create a life for me that was worth living.

I have had to do a lot of soul searching and learning through other people and experiences to understand who I am and where I am going.

Because of the intense experiences and emotions from my past, it was easy for me to slip back into old ways of being, repeat similar experiences in my life, go around in circles—and essentially miss the present.

Learning to accept me and my past and embrace my present and what is to come instead of fearing it has been a continuous but fruitful journey for me thus far. For me everything I knew had been removed from me so, in a sense, it could not get any worse. So what had I got to be afraid of? I felt I had just experienced a great removal and I was left with just me! This moment is where I had to learn that only I have the power to change my life, no one can do this for me. I am my creator and I must survive. I have to do this for my kids and my sister. I have to show people the greatness I have within me.

So here are some tips I've gathered along my path, to hopefully help and inspire you to live more holistically and presently…

- **See the past for what it was.**

Learning to accept your past is a process, and isn't always easy, particularly if it was traumatic or heartbreaking. First, you need to allow yourself to see your past for what it was. Acknowledge your thoughts and feelings, without judgment; there is no wrong or right way to do this.

As you unravel all there is to see and learn from your past, you may want to curl up in a ball and store it all away again; this is normal. Remember that accepting your past is not about wanting to change or forget about it; rather it is about altering your perception of it so that you can live more freely.

When I did this, I had to accept that my sister was not coming back. Although that was difficult for me, this initial step helped free me.

Since then, I have realised I still feel her around energetically, even though I cannot see her physically, and this is the most important thing for me. However, I could only experience that after I accepted her passing for what it was, and that took a good couple of years. The moment you begin to accept the past is the moment you begin your healing journey. This is the start of letting go, moving on, and living more for the present. Give yourself time. Remember that this is a process, not a race or a competition.

- **Tune in to your emotions.**

I can not express enough how important it is to allow yourself to feel openly and freely, regularly. Harbouring your emotions, particularly the negative ones, only brings more emotional turmoil and keeps you stuck in the past.

When my sister passed away, I often felt lonely and would hold on to that loneliness as a way of feeling closer to her. But I see in hindsight that this pulled me away from others and kept me stuck in a cycle of sadness and unrealistic expectations.

Share how you are feeling with someone close to you, whether it is a friend, family member, partner, or therapist; and if you do not have anyone close enough to do this with, let your emotions out through non-verbal means.

This could mean picking up your musical tools and playing some of your favourite songs, painting a picture, or writing a journal. Being creative is an exceptional and cathartic way of releasing anything that is stuck inside.

I did a combination of these things throughout my healing journey, and each one helped me become aware of my feelings, understand them, and let them go.

- **Practice mindfulness.**

Being mindful means being aware of your inner world (your thoughts, emotions, bodily sensations, breathing), and your outer world (your surroundings/environment, actions toward others) so that you can live more presently.

You can start a simple mindfulness exercise by focusing solely on your breathing; breathe for four seconds in, and four seconds out, and do this for about five minutes (you can do this for longer if you have more time).

This is a quick and fantastic way to calm or stop the chatter in your head and relax your body. And most importantly, it's a great way to bring you back to the present moment.

- **Observing your thoughts (and how they are making you feel) is another great mindfulness exercise.**

Our minds can conjure up so many different thoughts within seconds. Some of these thoughts can be positive, others can be negative, but most of the time our thoughts are past or future-oriented.

Our thoughts create our reality. The more you think of a particular thought, the more it becomes an ingrained belief, so it is important to be aware of your thoughts so that you manifest a positive reality, not one that is full of struggle.

For me, emotional pain manifested in health issues, and I enhanced my struggle by telling myself I could not get better. Through mindfulness, I learned to quiet these negative thoughts. While medical treatment helped improve my health, I know my mental state played a significant role in both my sickness and healing.

- **Being in nature can also pull you back to the present moment. Take half an hour out of your day to go for a walk or sit outside to be amongst the trees or your garden.**

Observe the sounds you hear—the rustling of the wind in the trees, the crunching sound of leaf litter, birds chirping, insects buzzing in harmony. Noting these things and the feelings or thoughts that come with these sounds can help you remember the beauty and simplicity of the present.

When I go for walks, I remind myself of these things: the ground is my soul, the trees are my natural beauty, and the sun is my inner radiance. Nature is a perfect reflection of who you are. Immersing yourself in it can be a confidence booster, as well as a beautiful reminder of how amazing you are.

- **Live your life consciously in the presen**t

Staying in the now and vowing to live your best life each day is a powerful antidote to a painful past. Say "good-bye" to the negativity as you let it go. Replace it with a positive thought or experience. Vow to stay in each moment to relish the beauty of everything you have that's wholesome and special to you.

- **Avoid letting anything stop you**

Even though you may still have contact with someone who has hurt you in the past, recognise that you hold all the keys to how your life journey continues from this point forward.

Making peace with your history is a highly rewarding experience. Learning to recognise and let go of the emotions connected with your trauma will lead to a more enriched life.

TELL ME. WHAT MADE YOU, YOU?

Write how your history has made you who you are:

Think about family, relationships, achievements... everything that
has made you the person you are today!

Look at your story with gratitude...

Thank the universe for your experiences and the lessons you learnt on the way.

FIVE
MOVING FORWARD

Moving forward is a relatively new and convenient way to indicate a progression in time from the present. The term suggests a continuing and progressive movement rather than, as the future can sometimes mean, some specific future date. **For me moving forward is more about reassessing where I am in the present moment and how can I navigate an easier way forward for me so that everyone involved benefits and as I say before everything I do... How can I do this with love**

TIPS ON MOVING FORWARD

Are you struggling to let go of the past and move forward? These tips will help you through this difficult process. Mistakes are a way to learn as we grow. Reflecting on past mistakes to make different decisions in the future can be beneficial!

Memories fade for a reason and details are forgotten. That mistake you made back ther might be distorted over time. Self-talk:

"I made that mistake. It's over. There's nothing I can do but move forward. Tomorrow is always fresh, with no mistakes in it."

- Lucy Maud Montgomery, Anne of Green Gables

Worrying is a trigger that tells you to fix something. Try planning (step by step) to identify any triggers and attempt to resolve those issues.

- Talk face to face with someone who has bothered you rather than through text or email. You will walk away feeling better about the conversation.
- If you find yourself dwelling on something, give yourself a time limit: "I will give this worry 10 minutes of my time, and then I'm done." Distract yourself with something new once the time is up.
- Plan out some healthy, positive, self-care goals to complete this week. Write them down where you can see them or set reminders on your phone. This will help you focus on the good in your life.

- Feel like you need closure but no longer have contact with someone? Write a letter to them and destroy it afterward. Or talk out loud as if they are in the room with you. It may sound weird but works as it is a great visualisation practice that is useful for pardoning as discussed previously.
- Reflect on situations that have resulted in hurt feelings. Is there anything you could have done differently? You can't change the past, but you can learn from it.
- It is natural for our minds to relive the past. When this happens, acknowledge the memory, forgive yourself, and refocus your attention to the **present moment.**
- Are you surrounded by an environment, things, or people that remind you of your past? Try to change it up; spend time in different places, donate things linked to bad memories and try to widen your social circle.
- **Remember that pain is not permanent.** The pain you are feeling right now will pass. Pain is a sign of growth. It will get better.
- Don't dwell on the negative aspects of the past, and instead focus on what is positive about the present. Try making a list of a few things in your life you are grateful for.
- If the uncertainty of the future is making you anxious, you might need some mindfulness techniques to help focus on the here and now so you can focus on doing your best today.

Letting go can be difficult. This guided meditation can make the process a bit easier.

Part of moving forward is making choices that are right for you. If you struggle to make decisions here are some tips:
- Is there someone who encourages and supports you? Take some time to thank them, whether it is a thank you card, surprise picnic, or a big hug. Focusing on the positive will take your mind off the negative for a while.
- Part of moving forward is trying new things. During this process, remind yourself that there is no right or wrong way to do anything. If you find a way that works for you, go for it!

- Your inner critic can be mean! Fight back and challenge your thoughts: "I know that I am great at these three things!" Having a more balanced view of yourself will help you move on with confidence.
- Are you overwhelmed by the thought of moving on? Put together a plan of action and break big steps into smaller steps. Try to do something each day to get you a little closer to your goals.

- You are the only person who has to live your life. You have control over your actions. Do what is right for you regardless of what people say. Doing something to gain approval will not make you happy in the long run.
- Sometimes fear can hold us back. Reflect on your fears: "What's the worst thing that could happen? What's the best thing that could happen?" Plan how you will deal with fear and then push through.
- Moving forward is hard work. Do the people around you bring you down or pump you up? If they bring you down, find some positive people to surround yourself with.
- Recognise that everyone is doing the best they can. If someone failed you or you failed yourself, recognise the effort and readjust your expectations. This will help you forgive yourself and others.
- Think about what you want to achieve in life. Try focusing on one goal at a time and break it into smaller steps. Having something to work towards will help you move forward.
- When you feel overwhelmed by change, don't give up; take a break instead. Engage in activities that are comforting and allow you to recharge.
- Focus on what you enjoy and try to determine if there is a way to make it a bigger part of your life. Do you like hanging out with adventurous people? Start rock climbing. Like cooking? Find a community kitchen or cooking class.
- Instead of focusing on what you can't do, focus on what you can do. This will help you feel like you are making progress.
- If you feel stuck, confused, and overwhelmed, take a short, brisk walk. Exercise and fresh air will do you good. You might be able to think more clearly afterward.

- Self-doubt can get in the way. Just remember you have what it takes to get through hard times and succeed. Go to my Youtube channel and listen to any of my 5-minute videos on how to get through where you are stuck now!

LET'S START MOVING FORWARD...

Write down what ways you'd like to move forward next to the numbers on the steps! This way, you can set your steps to growth!

10

9

8

7

6

5

4

3

2

1   Write goals here...

SIX

IMPLEMENTING CHANGE

Change is an inquiry that devours my musings consistently...

Could people in a general sense change what their identity is? How would you make a change inside an association? Would it be a good idea for me to change my work (once more)? Could you truly change the world? Would it be a good idea for me to change how I see and direct business? Would I be able to change myself? Are our characters liquid or are those default inclinations effortlessly changed? How would I change the alternate routes in my mind? How might I transform myself?

The topic of character, insight, and conduct (auto-activities), and routine play continually in my musings. To such an extent, that every one of the issues I work on appears to stream back to these subjects constantly.

So, these inquiries have driven me to what I accept is an equation for enduring change.

How about we consider them the 15C's.

15!? Indeed, I know, that is a great deal. At first, they were 5C's, then, at one point 7C's. Yet, as time advanced, I understood that more was engaged with a request to guarantee that the change is not impermanent. Genuine change can happen if there are sure conditions set up and if all regions have been thought about cautiously. What's more, if those conditions do not exist, we don't hang tight for them, we make them. The accompanying cycle has assisted me with carrying out an extraordinary, troublesome and perpetual change inside my outer work-life-conditions and my internal world-climate. I did not have this clearness from the start of the change cycle. It was solely after 1 to 2 and half years, that these pieces are clearer in my mind, and can be organised in a reasonable method to impart to you.

The 15C's

- Clarity
- Choice
- Commitment
- Courage
- Conditions
- Cause & Effect
- Calculate (Measure)
- Challenge
- Cultivate to Culminate
- Consistency
- Confidence
- Create more
- Consume less
- Contribution
- Collaboration

TIPS ON IMPLEMENTING CHANGE

It is not enough that we have to deal with the normal personal changes that we all go through in life. These days, however, we also have broader issues to contend with, such as the global economy, the domestic economy (job loss, company closures), the environment, technology, and changing cultural values.

As challenging and difficult as it may be, and as resistant we are to it, we have to learn to manage change.

It is in our best interests, however, to learn to accept change - even embrace it and welcome its challenges.

We can even come to terms with the fact that change can be good for us since it helps us develop and encourages us to grow.

Here are 5 Tips for Implementing Change:

- Take care of yourself. Managing change can be stressful if you are not prepared, so be sure to take care of yourself. Eat a balanced diet, exercise regularly, and get enough sleep. Take time to relax. When you are healthy, you are better equipped and in a better frame of mind to handle anything. If, on the other hand, you are already stretched to your limits and having trouble coping, change will only add to your difficulties.

- Be open and flexible. Knowing that change can occur at any time helps you accept and adjust to it when does happen. Be able to let go of expectations that no longer fit what is currently going on in the world. Certainly, at no other time in history has there ever been so much change or happening as rapidly as it is today. Even though most of us prefer to settle into comfortable predictable routines, realise that our current routine is probably temporary.

- Stay positive and put it into perspective. We all can control our inner and emotional responses to whatever happens. Our attitudes towards it and how we choose to deal with it are totally up to us. With that in mind, look for the positive outcomes of change - there are always some. How you react to it can often determine the outcome.

- Take control of your life. You can manage change by taking control of your life. Use your critical thinking skills. We all know that some change is forthcoming. Therefore, ask yourself what you can do in advance to help prepare for the transition. Make a list of options. Determine the best approaches. Take charge of your thoughts and actions. If you are mentally and psychologically prepared for change, it will not rock your world when it happens.

- Make changes. Become the change agent. Sometimes we are forced into making changes because we allow ourselves to get stuck in a routine or lifestyle that is no longer working for us. If, however, we anticipate it and become active rather than reactive, we can take control of a situation. We can look at where we need to make adjustments and then take action. Doing so can prevent the stress and anxiety that accompany unexpected change.

WE'RE IMPLEMENTING CHANGE

Implementing change doesn't happen overnight! Write down 3 small changes daily in the chart

below—these can range from selfcare to kindness toward others!

MON	
TUE	
WED	
THUR	
FRI	
SAT	
SUN	

SEVEN

PRESENT MOMENT AWARENESS

Being present-minded is the key to staying healthy and happy. It helps you fight anxiety, cut down on your worrying and rumination, and keeps you grounded and connected to yourself and everything around you.

Mindful of what? Mindful that you have been thrown out of the present moment. When you are present, you are in control. When you are not present, you have lost control. Everything happens inside. It is not that you are immune to external forces, only that when you notice that you are not present, you get back there.

Meditation, if practiced over some time, makes it much easier to be mindful and also to return to present-moment awareness. Yet you can also do a quick remedy by finding a quiet place to be alone, close your eyes, take some deep breaths, and find your centre again. Doing this several times a day is a good routine because it alerts you in a mindful way to what it feels like to be steady and present.

If you are present, here, and now, you are in control. The ego makes a mistake by always trying to get its way, putting up resistance, or being right. Countless people think of those things as being in control. In reality, nothing throws you out of yourself like demanding to get what you want, resisting other people, and always having to be right.

What we think in our minds will eventually become what we believe. This is why it is so important that we start saying positive things about ourselves many times each day. Choose two or three of the statements below and repeat them to yourself throughout the day.

(Feel free to highlight your favourites or write them down in a separate notebook or piece of paper.)

I LOVE MYSELF.

THE WORLD NEEDS ME.

I AM UNIQUE.

I CAN AND WILL DO THINGS TO PROMOTE HEALING IN MY LIFE.

I CAN HANDLE THIS ONE STEP AT A TIME.

THE SUN IS SHINING; I AM READY TO TAKE ON ANOTHER DAY.

MY PROBLEM HAS A SOLUTION; I WILL WORK ON A PLAN.

I AM A SURVIVOR.

I REFUSE TO GIVE UP BECAUSE I HAVEN'T TRIED ALL POSSIBLE WAYS.

I WILL INHALE CONFIDENCE AND EXHALE DOUBT.

I MAY BE ONE IN 7 BILLION BUT I AM ALSO ONE IN 7 BILLION!

I AM SMART.

I BELIEVE I CAN CHANGE THE WORLD (OR AT LEAST MY CORNER OF IT).

I AM IMPORTANT.

TODAY, I WILL CELEBRATE.

I MATTER.

I CAN FIND PEACE THROUGH PRAYER AND MEDITATION.

I AM STRONG.

MY CONFIDENCE IS BEAUTIFUL.

I AM IMPERFECT BUT I'M PERFECTLY ME.

MY SMILE CAN MAKE SOMEONE FEEL BETTER.

I CHOOSE TO FOCUS ON WHAT I CAN CONTROL.

EVERYTHING WILL WORK OUT IN THE END. IF IT HASN'T WORKED OUT YET,

IT'S NOT THE END.

I AM HAPPY WITH WHO I AM.

EVERY DAY, IN EVERY WAY, I AM BECOMING BETTER AND BETTER.

I AM A GOOD PERSON.

I KEEP GOING BECAUSE I BELIEVE IN MYSELF.

I CHOOSE TO SEE THE GOOD IN THE PEOPLE I INTERACT WITH TODAY.

IT IS ALWAYS TOO EARLY TO GIVE UP ON MY GOALS.

I CAN REACH OUT FOR HELP IF I NEED IT.

I AM SPECIAL; I WILL NOT CHANGE MYSELF FOR ANYONE.

I CHOOSE HOPE.

THE ANSWER IS RIGHT BEFORE ME, EVEN IF I DO NOT SEE IT RIGHT NOW.

I AM THANKFUL FOR...

I CHOOSE TO TAKE GOOD CARE OF MYSELF.

I ACCEPT MYSELF.

I CAN MAKE A DIFFERENCE.

MY PAST DOES NOT DEFINE MY FUTURE, I DO.

MY LIFE IS FILLED WITH POSSIBILITIES.

I REFUSE TO BE PUSHED BY MY PROBLEMS; I WILL BE LED BY MY DREAMS.

I AM AWAKE AND READY TO BE AWESOME.

I WILL FOCUS ON MY TALENTS; I HAVE THINGS TO SHARE WITH THE
WORLD.

I CHOOSE TO HAVE THE STRENGTH TO MOVE ON TO HEALTHIER
RELATIONSHIPS.

I DESERVE GOOD THINGS IN LIFE.

I RELEASE MYSELF FROM MY ANGER.

I LOVE WHO I AM.

I WILL ALLOW PEACE TO FILL MY SOUL.

TODAY IS A NEW DAY; I WILL SEE WHAT ADVENTURE IT HOLDS.

I CHOOSE TO BE PROUD OF MYSELF.

I WILL DO MY ABSOLUTE BEST IN ALL THINGS.

I WILL SPEAK KINDLY TO OTHERS AND MYSELF.

I CHOOSE TO BE BRAVE AND TELL OTHERS IF I NEED THEIR SUPPORT.

I HAVE THE POWER TO CONTROL MY REACTIONS TO THE CHALLENGES I
WILL FACE.

I AM BECOMING HEALTHIER EACH DAY.

I CHOOSE TO SEE EACH OBSTACLE AS AN OPPORTUNITY TO GROW.

I WILL STEP OUT OF MY COMFORT ZONE AND TRY SOMETHING NEW
TODAY.

I AM A SUCCESS; I CAN MAKE THIS A GREAT DAY.

NOTE TO SELF: YOU ARE AMAZING.

I CAN CONTROL MY BREATHING.

I WILL STAY CALM; IT WILL GET BETTER.

I ALLOW MYSELF TO FORGIVE; IT WILL ALLOW ME TO MOVE BEYOND THE PAIN, TO A PLACE OF PEACE.

I CHOOSE TO MAKE TODAY AMAZING.

I CHOOSE TO LET THE PAST GO AND MOVE ON TO THE FUTURE.

TODAY, I WILL BE COURAGEOUS.

I RELEASE ALL FEAR FROM MY MIND.

I CAN REACH MY GOALS, I AM UNSTOPPABLE.

I AM READY TO WRITE A NEW CHAPTER FOR MY LIFE.

I WILL TAKE THE TIME TO NOTICE AND BE THANKFUL FOR THE LITTLE THINGS.

I CAN WRITE DOWN MY THOUGHTS AND TAKE CONTROL OF MY EMOTIONS.

I AM A CHILD OF GOD.

MY HARD WORK IS ALREADY PAYING OFF.

I AM THANKFUL FOR LIFE.

I CHOOSE TO BE HAPPY.

I ACCEPT THE GOOD THAT IS FLOWING INTO MY LIFE.

I WILL NOT ALLOW ANXIOUS THOUGHTS TO STEAL MY JOY.

TODAY, I FORGIVE MYSELF.

MY BODY KNOWS HOW TO GET BETTER; I WILL LISTEN TO IT AND REST WHEN NEEDED.

I AM STRONGER THAN MY WORRIES.

I'M NOT THE ONLY ONE WHO STRUGGLES; I CHOOSE TO BE KIND TO EVERYONE THAT I MEET.

YESTERDAY WAS A BAD DAY, NOT A BAD LIFE. TODAY WILL BE BETTER.

I AM BRAVER THAN I FEEL.

WHILE I WAIT FOR THE STORM TO PASS, I WILL CHOOSE TO DANCE IN THE RAIN.

I AM LOVED.

I WILL REMEMBER, OFTEN DIFFICULT ROADS LEAD TO BEAUTIFUL DESTINATIONS.

THERE IS MORE TO LIFE THAN THIS MOMENT; I CHOOSE TO KEEP MOVING FORWARD.

I AM CAPABLE OF BRINGING MY DREAMS TO LIFE.

I AM OKAY. I AM BREATHING. I AM ALIVE.

I AM CAPABLE OF ACHIEVING GREAT THINGS.

I LIGHT THE WORLD WITH MY SMILE.

MY SPIRIT IS BEAUTIFUL.

I MAKE A DIFFERENCE IN THE WORLD.

I ALLOW MYSELF TO TAKE A BREAK AND DO SOMETHING I ENJOY.

I CAN SHOW KINDNESS TO OTHERS.

I'M NOT SURE WHAT WILL HAPPEN TOMORROW, BUT I'LL TAKE CARE OF MYSELF SO I AM STRONG ENOUGH TO FACE IT.

I CHOOSE TO APPROACH MY PROBLEMS WITH A CALM HEART AND MIND.

I TRUST MYSELF.

I WILL DO MY BEST WITH WHATEVER COMES MY WAY.

I HAVE A PURPOSE THAT I AM FULFILLING.

I WILL LISTEN TO THAT WHISPER OF HOPE THAT SAYS, 'YOU CAN DO IT, TRY AGAIN

I CAN CHANGE MY LIFE.

I WILL LEARN FROM YESTERDAY, LIVE FOR TODAY, AND HOPE FOR TOMORROW.

Speaking of worry, present moment awareness is a great way to cut down on how much you worry.

Follow these six steps to become more attuned to the present and rid yourself of excess anxiety:

Cultivate unselfconsciousness: let go and stop thinking about your performance. Practice savouring: avoid worrying about the future by fully experiencing the present.

Focus on your breath: allow mindfulness to make you more peaceful and smooth your interactions with others.

Find your flow: make the most of your time by losing track of it.

Improve your ability to accept: move toward what is bothering you rather than denying or running away from it.

Enhance your engagement: work on reducing moments of mindlessness and noticing new things to improve your mindfulness

SELF HELP TIPS ON PRESENT MOMENT AWARENESS

Do a 'Mindful Body Scan'

This straightforward exercise is an incredible method to get yourself feeling careful and reach out to your body. Doing this toward the beginning of the day can likewise assist you with getting your day away from work to a decent beginning. While sitting or resting on your bed (simply make a point not to nod off if you attempt this resting!), take a couple of profound, careful breaths. Notice how your breath enters and leaves your lungs.

Beginning with your toes, concentrate on each piece of your body in turn. Focus on how that region is feeling and notice any vibes that you are encountering. After a couple of seconds of centred consideration, climb to the following piece of your body (i.e., after your toes, centre around your feet, then, at that point lower legs, then, at that point calves, and so on)

This isn't just a decent technique for placing you in a careful state, it can likewise help you notice when your body is feeling unique in contrast to ordinary. You may get a physical issue or disease that you wouldn't regularly notice, just by requiring a couple of moments every morning to check your body.

Write in a journal / "Morning pages"

Another good exercise that can help you set the right mindful tone for the day is to write in your journal. A specific version of this exercise that is endorsed by author Julia Cameron is called "Morning Pages."

Here's how to use your journal as a stepping block to a more mindful day.

Early in the morning, before you head off to work or school or started checking things off your long to-do list, take a few minutes to pull out your journal or a notebook and make an entry.

You can do a new page each day and simply write however much you feel like writing, or you can try Cameron's Morning Pages exercise:

"Morning Pages are three pages of longhand, stream of consciousness writing, done first thing in the morning. There is no wrong way to do Morning Pages—they are not high art. They are not even "writing." They are about anything and everything that crosses your mind—and they are for your eyes only.

Morning Pages provoke, clarify, comfort, cajole, prioritise, and synchronise the day at hand" Whether you follow Cameron's guidelines or not, taking just a few minutes to write down any mindless "chatter" in your head or log any particularly insightful dreams can clear your head and help you start your day off in a mindful state.

Visualise your daily goals

Visualising your goals is a superb technique for not just making it almost certain that you will finish your objectives, it can likewise help you become more careful consistently.

At the point when you have defined your day-by-day objectives, take a couple of seconds to picture everyone.

See yourself undertaking every objective and finishing every objective today. Get as much detail as possible in your representation, so it feels genuine and inside your span.

At the point when you can see yourself scratching that everyday objective off your rundown, continue onward to the following objective and rehash until you have envisioned the entirety of your day-by-day objectives.

Rehearsing the perception of objective finish cannot just assist you with working on your concentration and care, it can likewise bring down your pressure, work on your presentation, upgrade your readiness, and give you the additional energy or inspiration you may have to achieve everything on your rundown.

Take a mindful nature walk

Taking advantage of the natural beauty around us is another acceptable method to develop greater mindfulness.

The following time you feel the requirement for a walk—regardless of whether it's a speedy excursion around the square or a protracted walk around a pretty, grand spot—make it a careful nature walk.

It is really easy to make any walk a careful walk; you should simply connect every one of your faculties and stay mindful of what is going on both around you and inside you.

Be deliberate with your mindfulness; notice your feet hitting the ground with each progression, see all that there is to see around you, open your ears to every one of the sounds encompassing you, feel each breathing, and breathe out, and just for the most part know about what is going on in every second.

This activity helps you associate with your real self; however, it likewise interfaces you to your current circumstance and works on your attention to the excellence that is throughout, simply holding back to be found. Add these advantages to the known advantages of strolling consistently—bringing down pressure, better heart well-being, and further developed temperament—and you have one helpful exercise!

Conduct a mindful review of your day

It can be easy to get tired and worn out by the end of the day and let things slip. To help you keep that mindful tone at the end of the day, try this exercise.

Towards the end of your day, perhaps after you finish all of your "must-dos" for the day or right before heading off to bed, take a few minutes to do a review of your day.

Think back to the start of the day and remember your mindfulness exercise that kicked it all off. Think about how it made you feel.

Think through the rest of your day, being sure to note any particularly mindful moments or memorable events. Take stock of your mood as you moved through your daily routine.

If you want to keep track of your progress towards greater mindfulness, it's a great idea to write all of this down in a journal or a diary; however, the point is to give yourself yet another opportunity to be mindful and end your day on the right note.

PRACTICING MINDFULLNESS

It's okay... I get it,

We all have busy lives, BUT putting aside 10 minutes a day for mindfulness can lighten the load!

Write out some 'simple mindful moments' you can add to your day-to-day!

EIGHT

WORKING ON YOURSELF

Working on Yourself means seeing that you are the most important person in your life, and knowing that when your needs are met, when you feel good, know your worth, understand the importance of your boundaries, be aware of your triggers, and know that being selfish with your growth means you restore a more healthy balance in all areas of living, all equals empowerment and freedom for you and means you can create that fulfilled life you believe is only a dream. It is not a dream, it can be your reality!

You do not need to be sick to work on yourself! The healthiest people in the world are often the ones who work the hardest on themselves - like Olympic Athletes. It is people who neglect themselves who are most at risk of getting sick. What is true for our bodies is also true for our spirits.

When our dreams are put on hold, it is common for resentment to build up towards the person whose needs are taking priority. We do not mind doing that for a helpless baby or an injured friend - but if we are doing it repeatedly for someone who could just as easily do it for themselves, our sense of injustice grows.

Over time, unchecked, that resentment has a way of creeping into everything we do. Like a poison spreading into our thoughts, our words, our body language, our tone of voice, our reactions. It is there and everybody can see it.

If - over a long time - our needs are not getting met, or our plans are repeatedly put aside while we are desperately trying to take care of someone else, it is hard to feel positive. We hold the abuser responsible for the abuse - but it is also common to begin to blame that person for everything that goes wrong - including the bad choices we have made too.

What happens when we blame someone else for everything bad in our lives? Hopelessness, helplessness and powerlessness. When someone else holds all the power - even though we may have given some of it to them - we eventually see no benefit to work on ourselves - after all, there is no point in building a house when you can see someone else lining up a wrecking ball.

Do you ever feel that way? - A sense that there is no point in working on yourself? That is despair - and it may be a sign that you have been neglecting your needs for too long, giving your power to someone else, and abandoning your past as the captain of your ship.

TIPS ON WORKING ON YOURSELF

- **Read Every Day**

Books are concentrated sources of wisdom. The more books you read, the more wisdom you expose yourself to. If you cannot read or do not like reading then audiobooks, podcasts or videos are amazing!

When you are reading a book every day, you will feed your brain with more and more knowledge.

- **Pick up a New Hobby**

Beyond just your usual favourite hobbies, is there something new you can pick up? Is there a new sport you can learn?

Your new hobby can also be a recreational hobby. For example, you can try baking, Italian cooking, dancing, knitting, creative design, etc. I take up a new hobby every year just for fun, not to be good at it, just out of curiosity and to take me out of my comfort zone! It really tests my brain, yet I love it when I start to accomplish small wins when I achieve anything in this adventure! I also get to meet new people away from my career field whom I learn so many new things from and learn different perspectives and opinions on life from. Yet most importantly I'm not there to impress them nor are they judging me, so I get to just be me!

Learning something new requires you to stretch yourself in different aspects, whether physically, mentally, or emotionally.

- **Create an Inspirational Room**

Your environment sets the mood and tone for you. If you are living in an inspirational environment, you are going to be inspired every day.

If there is a room in your house that looks messy or dull, take it to the next level by putting on a new coat of paint, buying a few nice paintings for the walls, or investing in some comfortable furniture to make it a space that will always feel welcoming and inspiring. A great and simple way to make a space more inspirational is by creating a vision board. By having a physical reminder of your goals and manifestations, it will be easier to visualise and focus on them.

- **Overcome Your Fears**

Whether it is the fear of uncertainty, fear of public speaking, or fear of risk, all your fears keep you in the same position and prevent you from improving your life.

Recognise that your fears reflect areas where you can grow as they act like a compass pointing at areas that need attention.

- **Wake up Early**

Waking up early has been acknowledged by many to improve your productivity and your quality of life. When you wake up early, you have more time to dedicate to self-improvement before everyone else is up. You will add extra time to your day, soak up the morning tranquility, and absorb the early-morning sunlight that will help your brain switch into its active mode.

- **Have a Weekly Exercise Routine**

A better you starts with being in better shape through physical activity. I make it a point to walk somewhere different at least 3 times a week, at least 30 minutes each time. Physical activity is also a great way to practise gratitude and self love to our body and all it does for us.

- **Write a Letter to Your Future Self**

Where do you see yourself 5 years from now? What kind of person will you be after you learn how to improve yourself? Write a letter to your future self and seal it. Make a date in your calendar to open it 1-5 years from now. Then, start working to become the person you want to open that letter.

- **Get out of Your Comfort Zone**

Real growth comes with hard work and sweat. Being too comfortable does not help us grow; it makes us stagnate. Identify where your comfort zone lines are and how you can begin to step out of them little by little. Go hiking on a trail you've never been to make a dish you've never tried, or say yes next time a friend asks you to go out when you'd normally say no.

- **Identify Your Blind Spots**

Scientifically, blind spots refer to areas our eyes are not capable of seeing. In personal development terms, blind spots are things about us we are unaware of. Discovering our blind spots helps us discover our areas of improvement.

- **Ask for Feedback**

As much as we try to improve, we will always have blind spots. Asking for feedback gives you an additional perspective as you learn how to improve yourself.

Some people to approach are friends, family, colleagues, a boss, or even acquaintances since they will have no preset bias and can give their feedback objectively.

- **Stay Focused with To-Do Lists**

Starting your day with a list of tasks you want to complete will help you stay focused. In comparison, the days when you don't do this can end up being chaotic or unproductive. You may forget certain tasks or end up running out of time since you have not created a plan to tackle each item.

- **Acknowledge Your Flaws**

Everyone has flaws, but what is most important is to understand them, acknowledge them, and address them through self-improvement practices.

What do you think are your flaws? What are the flaws you can work on now? How do you want to address them? Remember to do this with a sense of self-love. Do not look at your flaws in a self-critical or mean-spirited light. This is about finding areas you feel you can improve upon, not finding things that are wrong with you.

- **Learn From People Who Inspire You**

Think about people you admire, people who inspire you. These people reflect certain qualities you want to have for yourself as you learn how to improve yourself.

- **Get a Mentor or Coach**

There's no faster way to improve than to have someone help you achieve your goals.

- **Stop Watching TV**

Many programs and advertisements on TV are meant to distract you instead of empowering or educating you. This time is better spent elsewhere, such as with close friends, doing a hobby you enjoy, or exercising.

- **Start a 30-Day Challenge**

LET'S START WORKING ON YOU

What do you really feel is you?

To help distinguish the real you, let's scribble down some old habits and new practices!

The Old Me	The New Me

Set a goal and give yourself 30 days to achieve this. Your goal can be to stick with a new habit or develop a new hobby.

30 days is just enough time to strategise, plan, get into action, review, and nail the goal.

NINE
BELIEVE IN YOURSELF

Believing in yourself means having faith in your capabilities. It means believing that you CAN do something — that it is within your ability. When you believe in yourself, you can overcome self-doubt and have the confidence to act and get things done. Also, it means being able to trust yourself to do what you say you will do and knowing that those efforts will result in the desired outcomes. That means that believing in yourself comes from a mixture of several key psychological experiences—experiences like self-worth, self-confidence, self-trust, autonomy, and environmental mastery.

When we believe in ourselves, it kicks into gear all sorts of psychological processes that help us achieve our goals, manifest our dreams, and increase our well-being. But the flip side is also true. Lack of self-confidence or lack of belief in ourselves means we are less likely to act, to change, or to push to make things better. As a result, when we expect to fail, we are more likely to do so.

That means that believing in ourselves is kind of like the key that turns the ignition and starts the car. We can't go anywhere without it. Try as we might to push ourselves forward, we are blocked because our thoughts, attitudes, and actions are not in alignment with our goals. So, we either don't do what we need to do or we sabotage ourselves along the way, sometimes in obvious ways and sometimes in ways that are unconscious to us.

TIPS ON BELIEVE IN YOURSELF

To achieve anything in life, we need to maintain two conditions. Firstly, we must have faith that our efforts will bear fruit. Secondly, we must believe in ourselves. Faith is being sure of what we are hoping for and completely certain in things or situations that we do not see. Believing in yourself brings about self-confidence and strong trust in our abilities. With these two key elements intact, you can achieve anything that you want. Sadly, it is all easier said than done. With the various challenges that life sends our way, it is possible for us to lose faith and become hopeless. Moreover, bad experiences can leave us so damaged that we stop believing in ourselves. Should this happen, do not let up or give in. To stay strong here is how to cultivate the habits of having faith and believing in yourself.

- **Accept Your Current Situation**

The first thing you need to do if you want to get back up and start believing in yourself again is to accept your current life situation. You have to make peace with how your life looks at the moment and what led to this situation that you are in.

Fighting with your situation will not do you any good. Being resistant is pointless, so we must accept first. Only then will we have enough energy to change our life.

- **Think About Your Past Success**

If you are feeling down, use your past to get motivated again. Remember the time when you used to just kick butt. When you were awesome, and you used to rock it! Put yourself in that past and think about the amazing things that you used to do.

Now, remember that you can do it again. It is easy to think about the times when you got hurt, but it is just as easy to think about those times when you were successful as well. Use your past to your advantage.

- **Trust Yourself**

This is one of the most important things that can help you get that belief and confidence back. All the energy, power, courage, strength, and confidence is within you.

Spend time with yourself to access it, whether it be through meditation, journaling, or activities that make you trust in yourself again.

- **Talk with Yourself**

We are the ones who create who we will become. We do that every day by our daily beliefs and self-talk. We must talk to ourselves and motivate ourselves.

We ultimately don't need others' approval. You deserve your self-approval and supportive self-talk.

- **Don't Let Fear Stop You**

Fear stands for False Evidence that Appears Real. It is the main thing that holds you back from believing in yourself again more than anything else. Face your fears and do not let them stop you from achieving your goals

- **Let Yourself Off the Hook**

You have to forgive yourself for any failures or mistakes that you have committed in the past and move on.

You have to look at the future and stop living in the past. Be compassionate towards yourself.

- **Go with a Positive Attitude**

Having a positive attitude towards everything is the quickest way in achieving that belief and confidence in yourself.

Be thankful for whatever you are and whatever you have. Always have a positive approach and see the good in the world.

- **Let a Life Coach Help You**

A life coach is a professional that helps, supports, and guides you. A life coach can help you recognise your abilities and skills. They can help you refocus on your goals and remember your past successes.

When you are full of doubt, your life coach will believe in you and help you to believe in yourself again.

- **Keep Moving Forward and Never Look Back**

There are going to be countless times in your life when you will feel down, and you will feel like giving up. The voice in your head will tell you to stop and you will start to doubt yourself, but never listen to that voice. Be strong and keep moving on. Never give up on yourself. You have to keep on going and eventually, you will reach your destination. And when you do, you will realise how much more powerful you have become.

- **Let Life Move You**

Let your life follow its natural flow. When you learn to follow your life's flow, you will realise that life is marvellous and precious. If you let your life guide you, it will shower you with its gifts and riches. You have to accept the life you are given and you have to learn to relax. Allow it to let you move in the direction you are meant to go, and you will find success.

IT'S TIME TO BELIEVE IN YOU

Believing in yourself is ALWAYS the first step….

Write out your positive affirmation statements that reflect who you truly are:

Name:

Date:

You are worthy of your own self-belief! Namaste.

TEN
CREATING YOUR FUTURE

You can dream about it. You can plan it. You can try to make it happen. But you can never really prepare for the future unless you have a future-focused mindset.

Are you standing in the 'What's next?' doorway? Are you wondering what you should do with your life? So often we pull back from these pivotal moments unprepared to execute a plan — not because we don't want to change, but simply because we just do not have a plan. What you are looking for is a new vision for yourself—one that will ignite your spirit, fuelled by the energy within your heart — a new vision that will transform your life into a new reality.

Here are 6 ways to step forward to create a compelling vision for your future.

- **Slow Down**

All too often we focus on reacting to what is going on around us — the phone, the car, the job, the continuous pressing noise that surrounds our daily life. Stop. Hang it all up for a little while. Put aside time for yourself, to heal and adjust to your surroundings, to set a course for your future. Take some real time for yourself to just be by yourself for a little while, free from all the distractions in your life. Sit and think about what you want your life to be like and what you want it to represent.

- **Clear Your Mind**

Find a quiet place to be alone with your thoughts, to spend some time with your inner self. Take some deep diaphragmatic breaths in and out. Feel the air passing your lips while you clear your mind. When you arrive at a clear, open space in your mind, what do you hear? What is your inner voice saying to you? What is important to you, what are you passionate about, what are you great at? What is your true purpose in life?

- **Think Big**

Now is not the time to hold back; now is the time to let go. Think about what you are capable of and reach for the maximum outcome. If you aim high, your successes will be monumental. If you shoot too low, who cares, right? Take this time to dream about the possibilities and what you can do if you put your heart and soul into it. Truly step outside the norm and think about what you could accomplish if you bring your full self to it. Let go and dream about the possibilities for a while.

- **Get Focused**

Once you have a clear idea of what is important to you and what you are capable of, it is time to focus on what that looks like. See your vision for yourself in full detail, as if it were already completed. Imagine every single angle of this vision. Feel what it would be like to embody this image. Clarity is key; you must completely know what your vision will look like from front to back, side to side, inside and out.

- **Believe in Yourself**

Your spirit lies in your belief in the 'what if' and the possibilities of what you are capable of accomplishing. When you find yourself on the edge of self-doubt, stop and say: "Yes, I can do this. This is really who I am and who I am about to become!" Accept nothing less than your personal best for yourself and take things one step at a time. Small steps lead to giant leaps over time. Remember a time when you experienced success. Hold those thoughts and feelings close to your heart, and remember that you can do it. You have succeeded before and this time there is nothing stopping you.

- **Take Action**

Once you have developed your vision, you must take a step towards it to start the process of change. If not, you are just leaving another idea left to wash away and be forgotten. It doesn't have to be overwhelming — just a small step to symbolise the beginning of this next journey in your life. Prove to yourself that you are committed to making this a reality by serving yourself a taste of your future.

Remember, this is only the beginning. Time is ticking off right in front of you. What you do with your time shapes your destiny, so make every day count. Where you focus your heart is who you really are and what you will leave behind. What you do with your spirit will light up your soul forever. What you see with your vision is how you will live today and how decisions will be made for tomorrow. Visualise your future as rewarding and exciting, and recognise that your personal best is available to you!

CREATE YOUR BEST SELF
The life balance wheel

What do you desire and how much of that do you need to be your best self. Below is an example of a life balance wheel—a plain wheel is waiting for you to assist you in finding your perfect life balance.

Family

Friends

Career

Finance

Spirituality

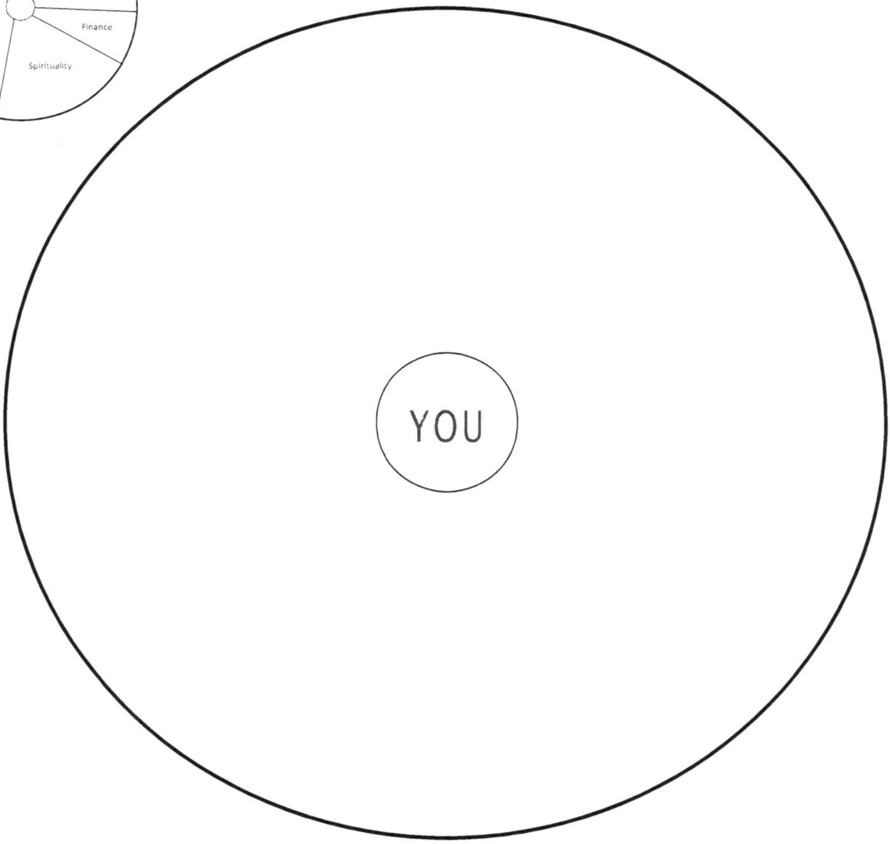

YOU

Everything you desire in balance...

PARTING WORDS

To everyone on a journey,

I hope my words have inspired you. Never give up on who you are and always believe everything will be ok.

Know you are your most powerful asset and know when you learn the tools for living... The journey is simply magical.

Create the life you want to live.

MEDITATIONS

I have compiled meditations and worksheets throughout this book!

Find them on my Youtube Channel here!

Printed in Great Britain
by Amazon

75249632R00035